Batman. Heads or tails

Batman™
Heads or Tails

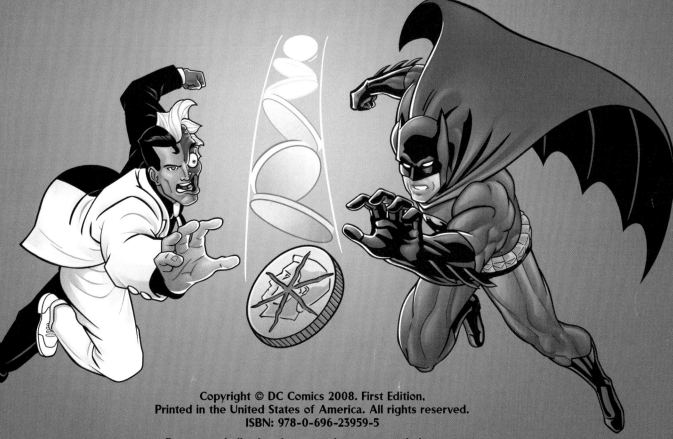

We welcome your comments and suggestions.
Write to us at: Meredith Books, Children's Books,
1716 Locust Street, Des Moines, IA 50309-3023

Visit us at: meredithbooks.com

Written by Brent Sudduth
Illustrated by Mada Design

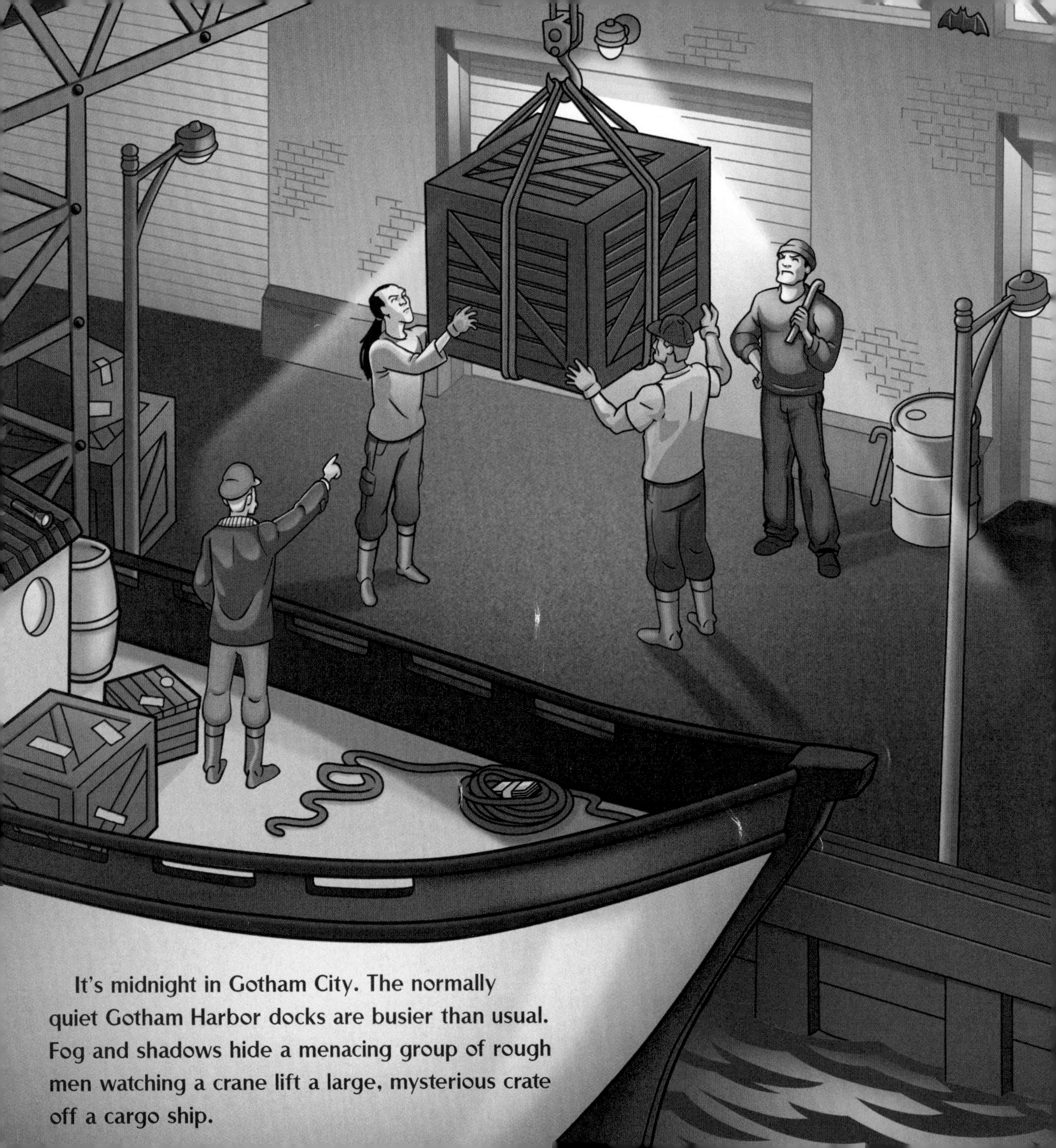

It's midnight in Gotham City. The normally quiet Gotham Harbor docks are busier than usual. Fog and shadows hide a menacing group of rough men watching a crane lift a large, mysterious crate off a cargo ship.

"Careful—or the boss is gonna be angry," whispers one of the thugs.

"I got it this far," the captain responds. "I can finish it."

Slowly, a strange black car pulls up. As the door opens, the rough men move back in fear. A tall, lone figure steps out.

"Fine work," says the man. "Especially you, captain."

"A-a-and you are . . . ?" the captain stutters.

"Two-Face," he replies. "I'm impressed you were able to get these past customs, captain. I've been waiting far too long."

"Two shipments of gold coins, worth $200 million!" Two-Face laughs, then points at the Captain and says, "Gentlemen, now."

"W-what?!" stammers the captain as two henchmen grab him.

"A classic double-cross, captain. Your services are no longer needed," says Two-Face, laughing.

Suddenly, two pellets drop and
smoke fills the damp air!
"Boss?" calls one of the
henchmen. "I can't see!"
"It's Batman!" Two-Face yells.
"Grab the gold!"

Under cover of smoke, Batman swoops in on a cable and carries the captain away.

"You'll be safe here," Batman calmly says to the nervous man. "But when this is over, turn yourself in or I'll come for you."

"I got the gold, boss!" says one of the goons, "I've got—??"

"Nothing," the Dark Knight whispers, cuffing him. "One down, three to go."

With a fast flip of his double-headed coin, Two-Face makes a decision. "Good side up—a good time to leave!"

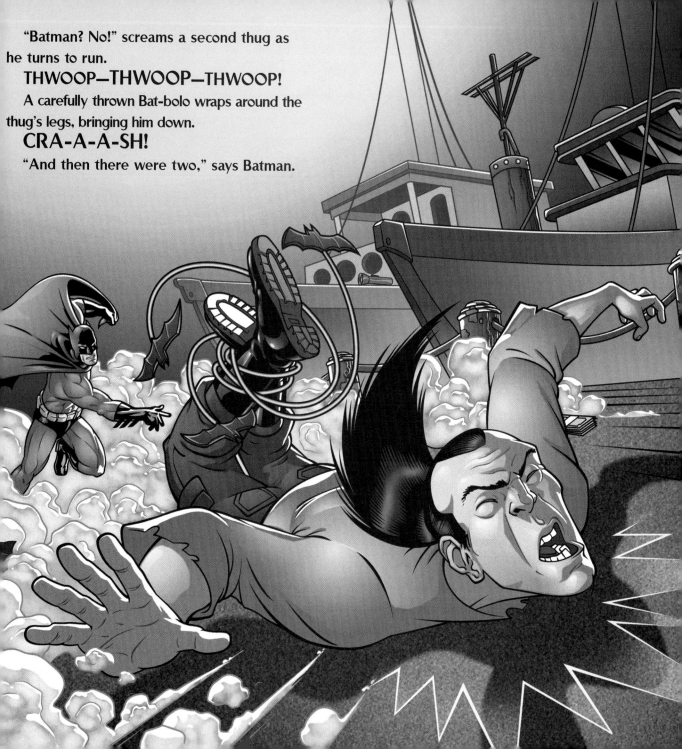

"Batman? No!" screams a second thug as he turns to run.

THWOOP—THWOOP—THWOOP!

A carefully thrown Bat-bolo wraps around the thug's legs, bringing him down.

CRA-A-A-SH!

"And then there were two," says Batman.

"We're not afraid of anyone," the Haney twins taunt.

Narrowly avoiding their grasp, Batman backflips into the darkness! With blinding speed a Batarang whizzes between the towering twins.

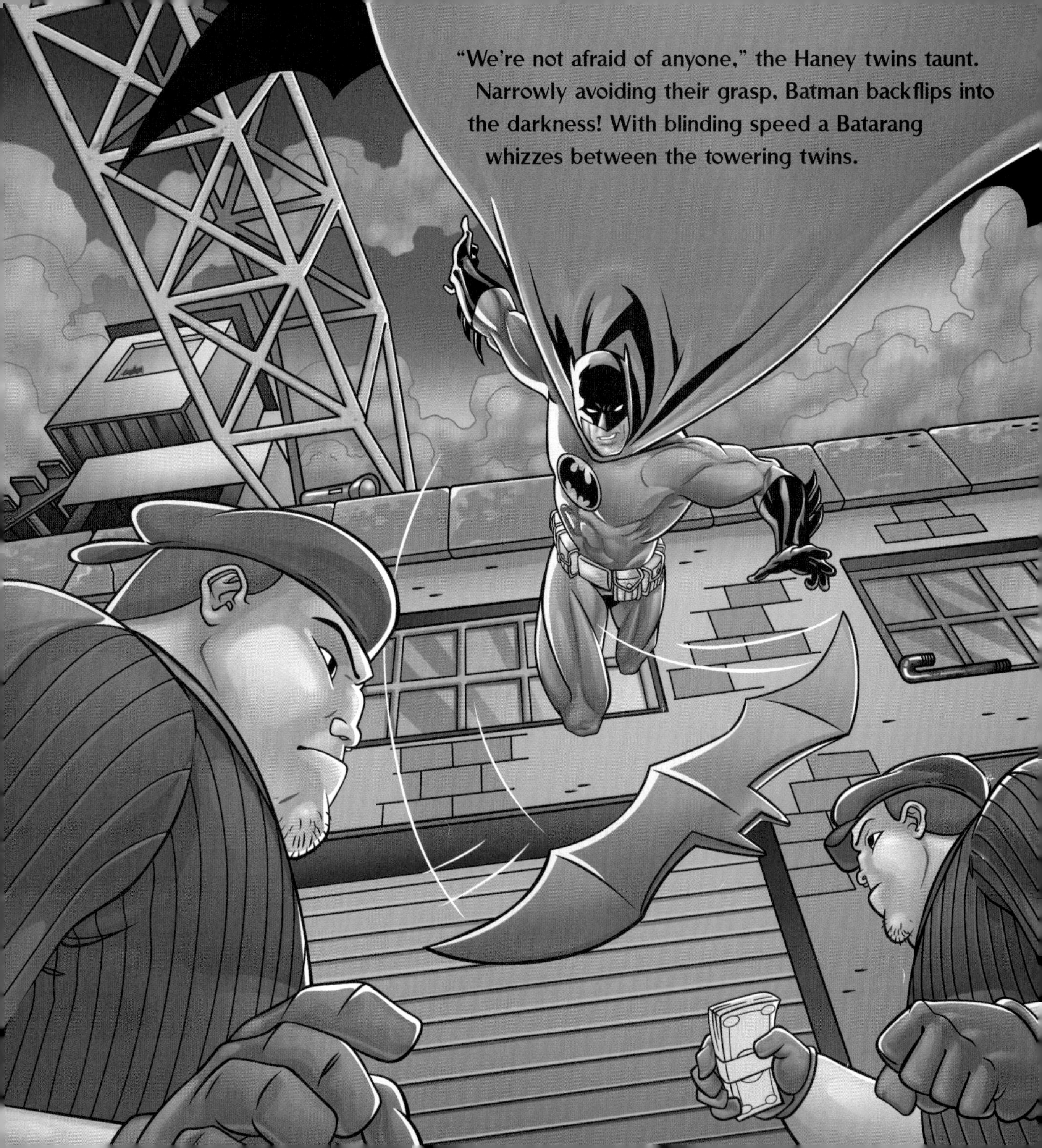

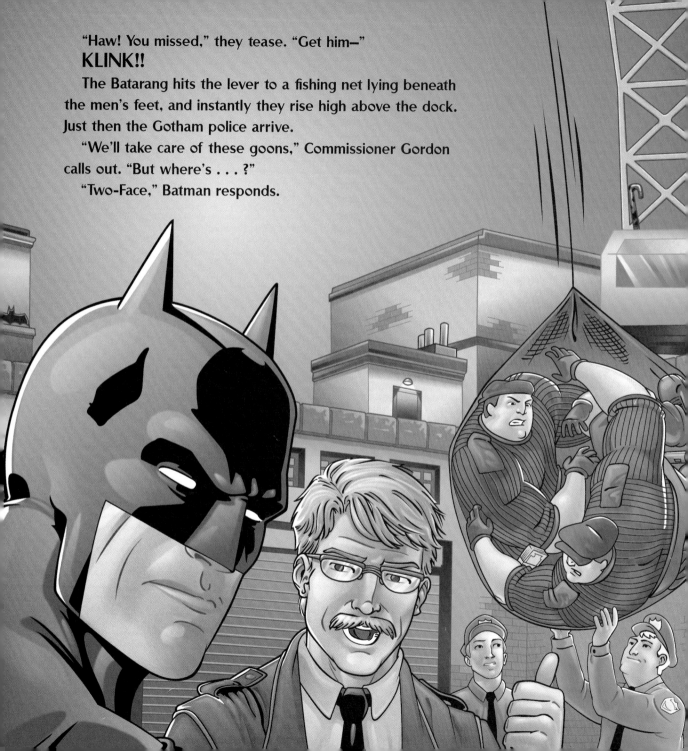

"Haw! You missed," they tease. "Get him—"
KLINK!!
The Batarang hits the lever to a fishing net lying beneath the men's feet, and instantly they rise high above the dock. Just then the Gotham police arrive.

"We'll take care of these goons," Commissioner Gordon calls out. "But where's . . . ?"

"Two-Face," Batman responds.

Two-Face runs until he has to stop. "Where do I go?" he wonders out loud as he looks around.

"To jail?" offers the Dark Knight.

"Too late, Bats," says Two-Face. But then—WHHZZZZ—a Batarang slams into Two-Face's hand.

"NO!" Two-Face yells as his lucky coin flies out of his hand! The coin soars high into the air and lands on a deliveryman's bike . . . bad side up!

"Ahhrgh!! Not more running!" Two-Face growls. "Bad for me!"

Batman follows, running along the rooftops. His hands reach into his utility belt for a grapple. Batman aims it just in front of the biking deliveryman.

"Gimme my coin!" yells Two-Face as he jumps the deliveryman.

CA-RAAAASH!!

This time the coin lands good side up. Two-Face cringes as he realizes that somewhere nearby has to be . . . !

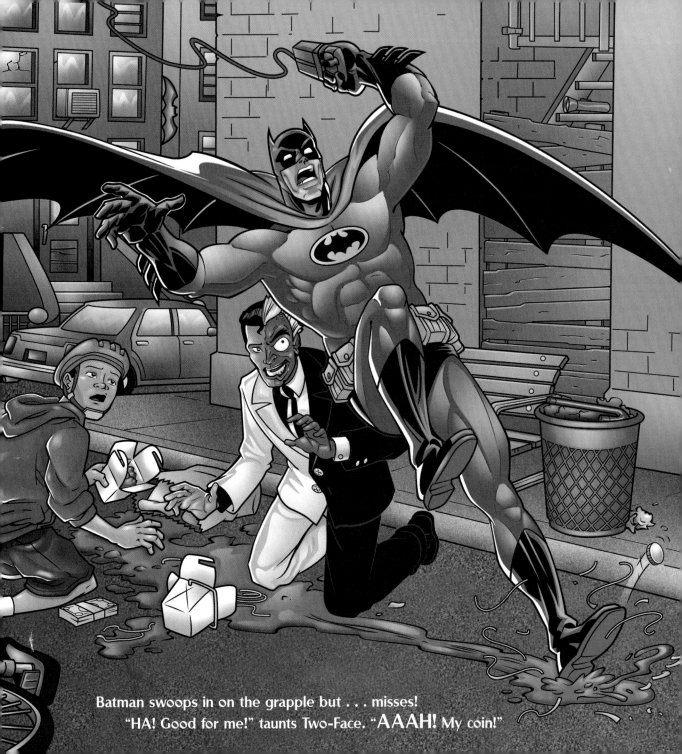

Batman swoops in on the grapple but . . . misses!
"HA! Good for me!" taunts Two-Face. "AAAH! My coin!"

Two-Face dives for the coin—
FLOOOP!

It shoots through the air, over a fence, and into a construction site. Two-Face scrambles after it as Batman bounds over the fence to cut him off.

he coin rolls out over a pit onto a long steel girder and
es to a stop standing on its side.
Mine!" Two-Face says, leaping toward the lucky coin.
No heads or tails?" says Batman, reaching the coin first.
can't have that," he says as he kicks the coin.

The coin rockets into a steel girder . . .

PING!

. . . and ricochets, nailing Two-Face squarely in the forehead!

THUNK!

Two-Face falls backward into a tub of fresh cement.

SPLAT!

"Batman! Did you find . . . ?" calls Commissioner Gordon as he runs up.

"His coin," Batman explains, "landed good side up."

Two-Face sits up and says, "But that would mean . . . "

"It's good for me," Batman says, finishing Two-Face's sentence.

Attention, Gotham City Crimestoppers!

Two-Face has hidden the items below throughout Gotham City. Batman needs your help finding them. Be careful! These items are dangerous and hidden on every page.